D0941268

Dedicated to my Grandma Daw
(without her this book wouldn't exist)

and to my Grammy who always
had a Tupperware container full
of dill pickles in her fridge.

-D.E.W.

www.BroomstickPress.com

Summary: Dill, a young cucumber, must decide if he will follow the trends and get pickled despite the dangers.

ISBN 978-0-9907384-3-5 (paperback) ISBN 978-0-9907384-4-2 (hardcover)

Keywords: [1. Pickles - Fiction. 2. Peer Pressure - Fiction. 3. Story in Rhyme - Fiction 4. Juvenile Fiction - Stories in Verse. 5. Cucumbers - Fiction. 6. Vegetables - Fiction. 7. Juvenile Fiction - Fables]

Library of Congress Control Number: 2018953593

DILL GETS IN A PICKLE

His name was Dillan,
but he went by Dill.
He lived in the tiny, old
town of Cukeville.

Dill was a quiet, but musical guy.
His songs even made tough cucumbers cry.

But Dill didn't have many friends at his school.
He wasn't popular, trendy, or cool.

One day Dill heard of a craze that was new–
getting pickled was now the big thing to do.

Dill overheard a kid say that he'd tried it.
When asked if it hurt, the same kid denied it.

He said that it cost him a whole lot of money,
and that after he did it he felt kind of funny.

Pickling for underage cukes was illegal;
t was banned 'cause it made their young bodies feeble.
But Dill thought, "If I follow the pickling trends,
more kids will like me. I'll have lots of friends!"

So Dill made up his mind to **get pickled** that day.
When his sister found out, she had something to say!

She said that his plan just didn't seem wise.
"Don't do it, Dillan!" she tried to advise.

But Dill thought,

And so Dill rode up to

the pickling place,

with **wobbly knees** and

cold sweat on his face.

HEY KID!
said the pickler.
His voice was gruff.
YER WELCOME TO LOOK, BUT DON'T TOUCH MY STUFF!
CHIP
Dill saw glass jars and bottles
that bubbled with brine,
and simmering tubs that
sent chills up his spine.
NO WIMPS BEYOND THIS POINT
FIRST TIME FREE!

WELL, WHADYA WANT?
the old pickler growled.
When he saw Dill's reluctance, he grunted and scowled. The butterflies turning in Dill's stomach tickled.
His voice cracked when he said,
SIR... I'D LIKE TO GET PICKLED.

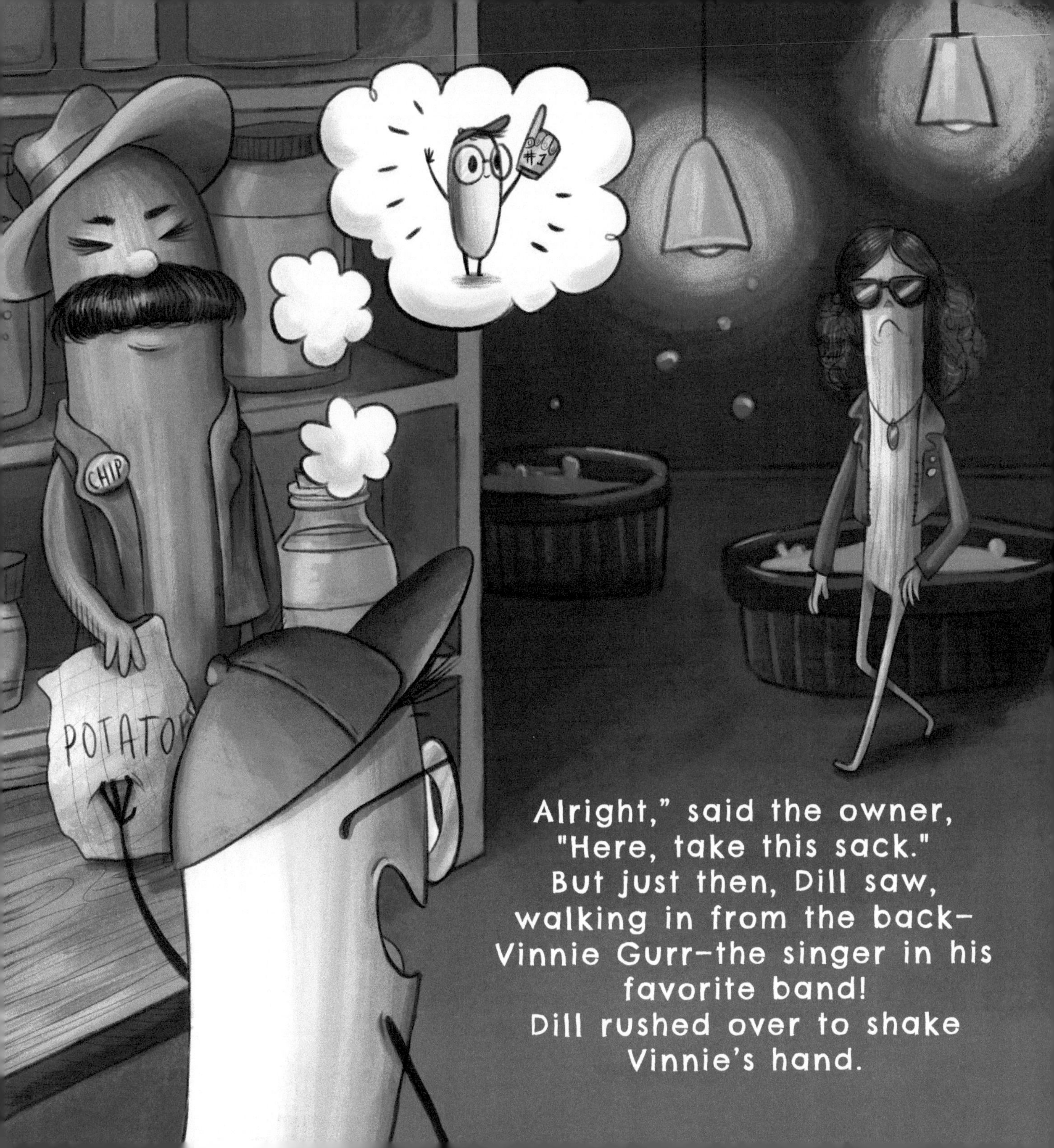

Alright," said the owner,
"Here, take this sack."
But just then, Dill saw,
walking in from the back–
Vinnie Gurr–the singer in his
favorite band!
Dill rushed over to shake
Vinnie's hand.

But when he got close, he saw Vinnie was wrinkled.
His long hair was matted; his jacket was crinkled.

Dill caught a whiff of a horrible smell.
It was coming from Vinnie, Dillan could tell.

Dill asked Vinnie, "When's your next show?
I'm your number one fan, and I'd love to go!"
Vinnie said sharply,
KID, GET OUT OF MY WAY! I'M LATE AND I NEED TO GET PICKLED TODAY!

Vinnie had always been
such a cool guy.
But now he was different
and Dill wondered why.
Getting pickled must have
caused Vinnie to change.
That's why he looked, smelled,
and acted so strange!

Suddenly Dill knew his sister was right–
wanting to make friends had blinded his sight.
Now Dillan found himself in a bind.
He must tell the pickler that he'd changed his mind.

Dill courageously said.

The owner then snarled,

He had worn out his welcome at the old pickler's store.
Without saying goodbye, Dill ran out the door.

The next day, when Dill told
his classmates the tale,
that he'd almost been pickled,
one kid's face went pale.

The kids were all shocked at the dangers he'd faced,
and thanked Dill for warning them to stay away from that place

Then an idea popped into Dill's seeded head.
"I know of a way to warn others!," he said.

"I'll start a **band**
to teach younger cukes.
My band mates will sing
and strum on their ukes!
We'll tell of the hazards of pickling through song,
and show other kids that it's
harmful and **wrong**."

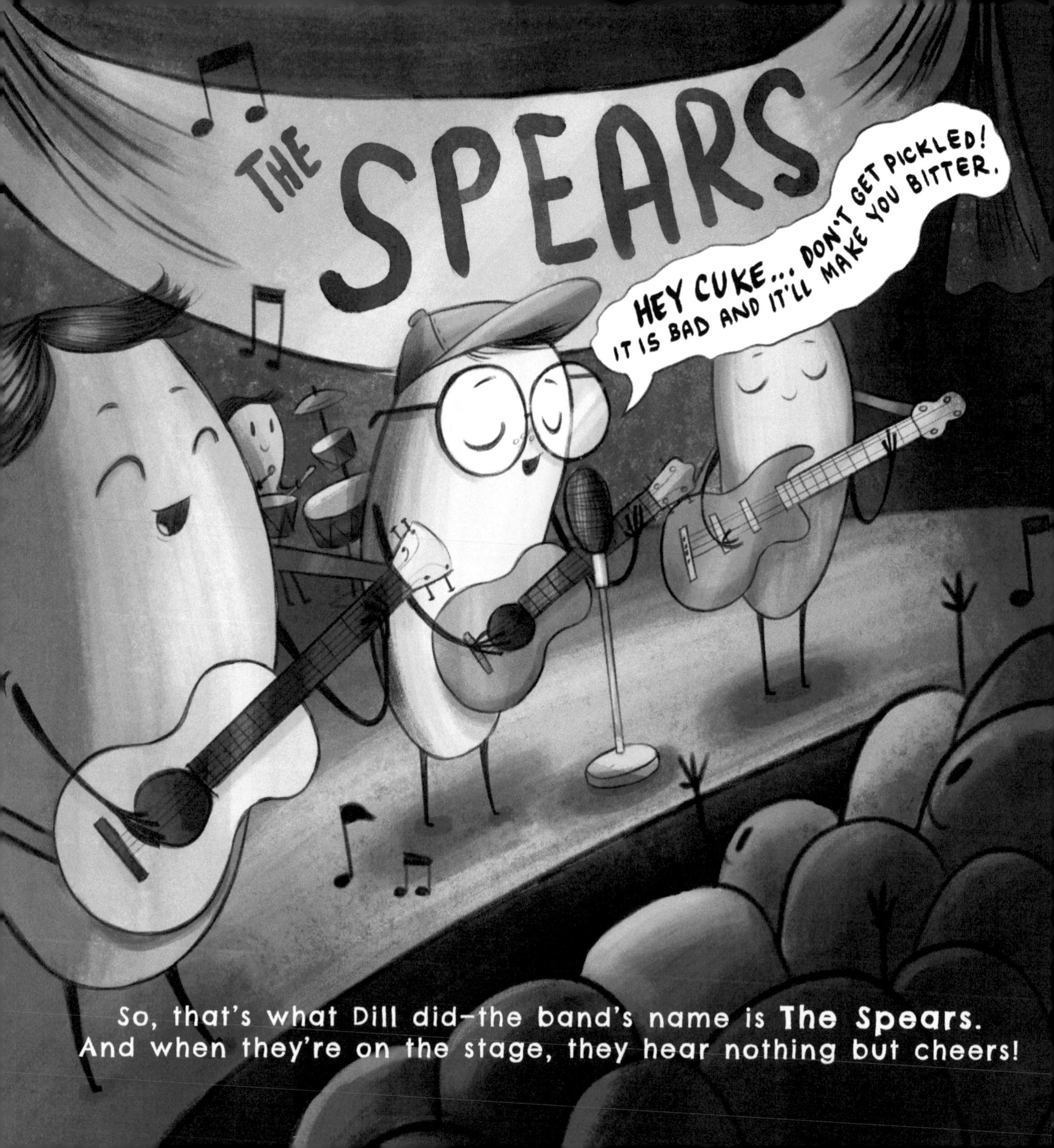

So, that's what Dill did–the band's name is **The Spears**.
And when they're on the stage, they hear nothing but cheers!

Now **The Spears** are on tour– they play sold-out shows.
And day after day their following grows!

DANIELLE ELISON WEBB

enjoys writing children's books, song lyrics, and short stories. But she doesn't enjoy writing to-do lists or anything serious. She wrote the lyrics for the award-winning children's song, "Could You Ever Love a Witch?" and one of her short stories was published in a magazine with national distribution. Danielle loves pickles - dill flavored only. She would like to thank all the cucumbers that were pickled for her consumption. They're the inspiration for this book!

ASHLEY FAIRBOURNE

is a freelance illustrator who prefers to focus on the quirkier side of life. She is pretty good at crocheting, weirdly good at freestyle rapping about her dog, and not so good at keeping a straight face in photos. When she isn't doodling, she enjoys playing music & baking. Ashley is based in Salt Lake City, Utah.